Annabel
on the trai
where you're i...
the Great Fire!

love Poco x

TINY TREE
CHILDREN'S BOOKS

First Published 2018

Tiny Tree (an imprint of Matthew James Publishing Ltd)
Unit 46, Goyt Mill
Marple
Stockport
SK6 7HX

www.tinytreebooks.com

ISBN: 978-1-910265-77-2

Printed by Chapel Print Ltd
ROCHESTER | www.chapelprint.com

FOR MARTHA AND STANLEY

"You see, you placed the Star of Wonder behind the face of Time.
Wonder was hidden by Time."

THE FORBIDDEN KEY

Sidney looked at the forbidden key. It was on a level with his nose, and if he reached his arm up he could finger its dull metal. Without quite meaning to, he found the key was turning sweetly, and the longcase door opened, making no noise. He peered inside. A pendulum swung and ticked and below hung two weights on pulleys. Beneath them was a deep darkness, and a smell of dust. He stood completely still, and after a moment let out his breath in a gasp. It was the perfect place. He darted over to his school bag propped against the wall and fumbled in its depths. Out came a silver star, shiny with spangles and glitter. All remained quiet in the hall, so he took the star and hung it over the darkness in the clock. Then he let it fall, hidden and safe. He pushed the conker-brown door closed and turned the key.

'I'll look after it, Miss,' Sidney had said to his teacher the week before, 'till it's the Nativity.'

'Alright,' she said, unwilling to disappoint him, and pushed away the heavy fringe from her tired face. He carried it around in his bag all week and it was starting to look a bit battered. Sidney found Mark rummaging in his bag one day at playtime and swiped him across the face. Mark yelled, Sidney was kept in and Mark stuck his tongue out at him through the window. But no one would ever find the star hidden in the grandfather clock at his Grandpa's house.

'Sidney!' He jumped and the key fell on to the carpet. The living-room door jerked open. 'What are you doing? You're not messing with that grandfather clock again are you?' Sidney shrugged but without giving his mother eye contact.

'Hurry up and get ready! We're going to meet Mark and his Mum at the Garden Centre.'

Sidney looked over his shoulder just in time to see the brass clock face gazing back at him, and heard the tick-tock of the pendulum hidden inside the longcase.

At the Garden Centre was noise. Jingle Bells blared, and Sidney forgot about the star. He and Mark raced around, played tig and dodged tutting shoppers. Everywhere was an ice-cave, with lights that glittered like frost, fake snow on the trees, baubles, silver spangles, polar bears, snowstorm globes, feathered doves, penguins, and glass icicles all in a glorious evocation of winter. The Snowman and The Snowdog floated on enormous screens, their haunting music a backdrop to the loveliest supporting cast of

Christmas. Sidney stopped to watch, and suddenly something about the melting Snowman frightened him.

'Mum.' He tugged her arm. 'Mum, suppose I lose the star?'

'I thought it was safe in your school bag?'

'Yes. But I put it in a safe place.'

'What for?'

He hung his head, and she caught the glint of a tear.

'Come on then. Let's find another one and I'll buy it for you. Just in case.'

So the two families set about finding a glittery star. They searched and searched. Even Mark made an effort to look. But in the end they gave up. There were no stars, apart from some tiny chrome ones that were hollow in the centres. There were no shepherds, no sheep, no kings with gifts, no angels, no stables, no Mary, no Joseph, no baby Jesus to be found in the store. It was just as if the Christmas story had been airbrushed from the shelves. They asked an assistant who said, 'Nativity? Well everything for sale's been put out.'

Sidney rubbed his face and left a dirty trail down his cheek with his thumb.

'Tell you what,' said Mark's mother 'let's buy you two boys a drink and a chocolate cake.' Sidney and Mark whooped with excitement. For the moment the star was forgotten.

Next day was Sunday, and Mark and Sidney went with their mothers to a National Trust House with a special Christmas Trail that searched out the Twelve Days of Christmas.

'Bet you can't find four calling birds,' said Mark. His hair stood up in brown tufts all over his head and his teeth needed brushing.

'I can.'

'Bet you lost that silver star Miss gave you to look after.'

Sidney turned bright red. 'I haven't!'

'Why d'you say you couldn't bring it to school then? Miss asked you to bring it and you said you couldn't till next week.'

'I haven't lost it!' Sidney was shouting now.

Mark ran on ahead to the old stable block. He turned round and pulled a face.

Sidney tore after him. 'I've put it in a safe place. Safer than you would!'

'Well, my star's better than yours!'

'You haven't even got one.'

Mark glared. 'Miss bought another one. I heard her say, "Just in case" and she's put it up on top of the cupboard, so you won't get it.'

Tears poured from Sidney's eyes. 'She's going to use mine. I made it and I'm doing the special part at the Nativity!'

'Cry baby! Cry baby!'

The two mothers rounded the corner to see their sons in a heap on the ground. Feet kicked. Fists punched. Hair got pulled. Eventually they managed to part them.

'Say you're sorry. Both of you.'

After a moment mutterings were heard, and the two boys were dragged into the stables display.

'Why couldn't Mark be friendly, just for once?' Wondered Sidney.

'You'd better make sure you look at the Four Calling Birds, or we're going straight home,' said Sidney's mother, her cheeks pink. She gave him a good shake that somehow ended in half a hug. He dragged himself over to the four birds, tiny, and made out of dull grey tissue paper. They were hanging from threads so they could pirouette in the draught.

'They aren't calling,' said Mark, but no one looked at him.

'Oh,' said Sidney's Mum who was reading a leaflet, 'that's interesting.'

Three pairs of eyes fixed themselves on her face.

13

'It's an old word. It's "colly" not "calling". It should be "Four Colly Birds."'

'Colly?'

She read on. 'Colly – short for colliery.'

'Four colliery birds? Like canaries?' asked Mark.

'No,' said Sidney suddenly. 'Black as coal dust. Colly birds are black. It means blackbirds.'

Mark frowned and wandered off. His mother checked her mobile while Sidney's Mum put on some lip gloss. Sidney fixed his attention on some old engravings displayed on a table nearby. A group of children stared back, blank-eyed, with matted hair and strange clothes. Some had faces so black with coal dust that their teeth gleamed white.

'Oh, those poor Victorian children,' breathed Sidney's mother. 'They must have worked down the local pit. They were called trappers and had to sit for hours pulling the trap door open with bits of string.'

'What happened to them?' asked Sidney.

'The colliers pushed their carts of coal past them on little railway lines. Once they'd gone, the candlelight went with them. The trappers had to sit for hours in the dark all day.'

Sidney's hand crept into his mother's.

'It's not that long ago really.'

'It must have been really scary.' Sidney said thoughtfully.

'Not much Christmas for them, then,' said Mark's Mum.

Later, in the car back home, Sidney and Mark sat in silence. Suddenly Sidney felt Mark's hand on his arm. He looked up. Mark was offering him a white sugar mouse.

'Soz,' he mumbled.

'Ta,' said Sidney and grinned. They slept.

The week passed in a whirl of rehearsals. Nothing more was said about Sidney's star. The teacher produced a different, shop-bought one for them to practise with. His Mum bought one she'd found at the Newsagents with bright pink glass jewels stuck all over it. She left it at the Secretary's office, where it remained in a plastic bag under the desk. On the Saturday morning Sidney and all his family drove to his grandparents' house.

'I'll find a moment,' thought Sidney, 'and slip my arm into the long-case, feel for my star and hide it in my school bag again.'

They spilled into the hall and his grandpa met them, unsmiling.

'It's taken me days to find that key,' he said. 'It'd fallen out of the keyhole, I've no idea how. And it got kicked underneath the case.'

Four pairs of eyes stared down at Sidney. His sister, Mandy, smirked. His father's eyebrows were drawn together in a frown.

'I didn't…I didn't…I…sorry.'

'And,' went on his Grandpa, 'it chimed ten o'clock twice and then stopped altogether. I just can't understand it. So I've had to take it to the clock-menders.'

Silence fell. All his family stepped back and made an empty space on the carpet. Sidney stood alone. He gazed up at the clock. This time it didn't gaze back. The clock face had gone! The 'hood' was blank, empty behind the pane of glass. The door hung open. There was no pendulum. No weights. No tick-tock. No chimes. Everything that made a living clock had gone, as if the real clock had died and left a shell behind. Sidney threw himself onto the settee and sobbed. All anyone could hear was the word, 'Star'. Grandpa had a good look and shook his head. Not only had the clock gone, but now the star had gone as well.

After some whispering Grandpa said, 'How about coming into Alderley with me, Sidney? We'll go and ask the clock-mender if he's found your star.'

Without a word Sidney nodded.

As they drove along Grandpa said, 'Alderley is a village of mystery.' To take Sidney's mind off things he began to tell him tales of wizards, and of King Arthur's knights who slept, so legend had it, underground in caverns beneath The Edge until they wake to fight for Britain in her hour of need. 'People say they've seen them sometimes.' He laughed, 'Usually at dusk, when the light's going.'

'Have they really seen wizards? With pointed hats and wands?' Sidney sat bolt upright, the clock momentarily forgotten.

Grandpa shrugged. 'I don't know.'

Sidney snuggled back in his seat and stared out of the car window. What if he were to see a wizard on The Edge one day? Maybe he and Mark could have an adventure one twilight evening when the grown-ups were busy?

Grandpa parked the car at the side of the road. 'Look.'

Sidney lifted his head and saw a cobbled street that wended its way through terraces of houses. The sun shone through mist that lingered and turned it golden, while The Edge reared up its head beyond, brooding and flattened in shadow.

'Come on, let's see Mr. Humble.' Grandpa rang the bell and the front door opened. A man, so bent, grey and lined, stood there and smiled at them. He had teal-coloured eyes and shuffled in slippers. Sidney wondered if he were the wizard. Chimes came rushing out from behind him into the garden, different in tone and timing. Some boomed and some were silvery.

'Come in. The workshop's this way.'

They crowded into the front room and Sidney wrinkled his nose. There were clocks everywhere.

'This one plays a tune,' said Mr Humble and wound it up. A Viennese waltz of the nineteenth century spilled off-key into the room. After a while it stopped and Mr Humble sighed. Everywhere was messy, thick dust on the benches and old pots stuffed with tools, nearly all long and thin.

'Please, sir, I've lost my star.' said Sidney

'Oh, dear.'

'I hid it in the clock.'

'I see.'

Mr Humble limped across the carpet to a wooden stand. At the top was attached a brass face, with weights and a pendulum.

'Now, where did you hide it?'

'I let it fall inside.'

'Ah. Maybe it fell onto one of the weights as it descended,' said Mr Humble. He prodded and poked, sat down and stood up, peered into a waste paper basket and delved into it once. Then he began to feel carefully at the back of the clock face. It was very quiet.

'Is this it?' He eased out a silver point from amongst the cogs and wheels behind the brass face. Slowly, slowly the star appeared, its glitter and spangles catching the sun.

Sidney yelled, 'It's mine! That's it!' He flung his arms round Mr Humble's knees. 'Thank you.'

Mr Humble sat down rather suddenly. 'Did you make it?'

'Yes. I've got to hold it up at the Nativity and tell everyone in a very loud voice that they've got to follow the Star of Wonder. And I lost it and the grown-ups got angry and told me off.'

'Well, young man, it's found now. And you did hide it in rather a special place.'

Sidney gazed up at him.

'You see you placed your Star of Wonder behind the face of time. Wonder was hidden by time.'

Sidney glanced across at his Grandpa but all he did was smile broadly.

'You see The Edge up there?' Mr Humble pointed through the window. 'People tell lots of tales, but I've been up there and watched the stars at dead of night. They wheel and dance around the skies like clockwork, like my clocks telling us the time. But don't forget. Behind it all is wonder. There's a Star of Wonder hidden from view unless you search for it.'

* * *

On the Tuesday before Christmas Eve Sidney stood in the darkened school hall. The atmosphere was hushed and expectant.

'Here is the star, Oh Kings,' he cried. He carried it high, climbed onto the stage, held it aloft, turned and pressed its Velcro onto the top of the stable roof. It stuck there, only slightly askew. Behind him came the three Kings with cardboard camels, one held by Mark. The Kings pointed and nodded their foil crowns. Sidney moved into the limelight and opened his mouth to sing.

'Star of Wonder, Star of Night, Star with royal beauty bright, Westward leading still proceeding, Guide us to thy perfect light.'

Later, while Alderley slept, the clock-mender opened a bottle of sherry and took down a dusty glass. Mark snuggled under his duvet, Sidney snored and Grandpa patted his newly oiled clock. And seen from The Edge itself, the stars of the Milky Way made a path right across the heavens.

THE GLITZY GIRLS

It was so unfair. Mum was mean. Mandy flounced up the steps at the side of the theatre. Stage Door she read, and plonked herself down on the second step.

'She'll never find me here,' she thought. 'She can look and look. And then, when she's really upset and thinks I'm lost, I'll walk across the stage, bow to everyone, wave at Mum and blow her a kiss.'

Even Mandy realised that this was an unlikely scenario. The cold of the stones began to seep through her coat, skirt and tights and made her shiver. She looked down towards the end of the street. Red tail lights from the cars flashed past, the sound of carols played by a brass band floated on the chilly air, and a thousand white fairy lights winked in the bare branches of trees. In the distance a siren sounded. But down here the side street was in dark shadow and a cold wind swirled.

Mandy got up and rubbed her knee, which ached a lot today. Across the street was an old man who pushed a barrow. A sweeping brush was standing erect inside it along with a shovel that clanked. He had a pole with a sharpened iron end which he darted into old crisp packets and chocolate wrappers. Mandy called out to him but he didn't seem to hear her. She stepped into the road, remembered school warnings and stepped back onto the pavement.

A girl was walking briskly down the street towards Mandy. She stopped at the bottom of the steps and looked up at the pre-teenage girl with the dark curls and wide-eyed look.

'Hello.'

'Hello,' said Mandy, 'what's your name?'

'Jazz.'

Mandy stared blankly.

'Jazz. Short for Jasmine.'

'The same as The Glitzy Girls,' said Mandy with her extra loud laugh.

Jazz didn't reply at first. Then she said, 'Are you with your Mum?'

Mandy shrugged. 'Yes, but she's being mean to me.'

'Mean?'

'She won't let me stay behind afterwards. I wanted to talk to The Glitzy Girls after the show, but she says it's too late and Sidney needs to get to bed.'

'Oh. And who's Sidney?'

'My little brother. You're wearing nice trainers.'

Jazz said gently, 'I think you ought to go back to the front of the theatre now.' She glanced at her watch. 'There's just time. I'll take you.'

'Did they cost a lot of money? I'd like some with pink sequin stars on. Mum says she hasn't got any cash.'

Jazz recognised delaying tactics when she heard them. 'Come on now.' There was an edge of firmness to her voice.

'But I might see one of The Glitzy Girls coming in at the Stage Door.'

'You can't use the stage door.'

'Why not?'

Jazz began to worry about the time. She pulled off her woollen hat and long golden hair cascaded out round her face and onto her shoulders. The man with the barrow had crossed the road and boxed them in at the bottom of the steps.

'Oh, Lonnie, do move on,' cried Jazz. 'No one can move up or down with you there.'

'Only doing my job, Miss.' He leered at Mandy's tights.

Jazz made up her mind. She pushed Mandy up in front of her, jabbed a number into the keypad on the door so quickly that it couldn't be seen from behind and swept the girl into the back of the theatre. She slammed the door shut behind them and cut out Lonnie's open mouth, slack with surprise.

'Upstairs!' she ordered Mandy, who turned to linger and chat, but found instead she was galloping up the steep stairs, up and up until she was puffed and her legs ached.

'I'll worry about you in a minute,' said Jazz. She plonked Mandy onto a chair, slung some teenage magazines in her direction and flew out of the dressing-room. 'Wait till I get back.' And with that Jazz was gone.

At the front of the theatre a crowd had grown. A red-haired woman paced the foyer, jabbered and gesticulated into her mobile. There was a siren that grew louder and louder until a Police car screamed up, slammed on its brakes and left the blue lights flashing. Seconds later another one arrived from the opposite direction. Six uniformed officers leaped out and fanned in all directions around the theatre.

'Ten year old girl missing,' cried one into his phone.

A PC strode up to the red-haired mother and led her by the elbow towards the manager's office.

'Mrs Curtis? Dina? Come out of the limelight and tell me what's happened.'

Dina allowed herself to be led away but suddenly stopped and craned her head round. 'Where's Sidney?'

'Here, Mum.' Sidney materialised at her side. 'Mum, she went that way.' He pointed to the side of the theatre and the maze of streets in deep shadows. He set off again but his mother grabbed him by his jumper.

'Please don't you get lost as well.'

'But I can help you find her. She'll be frightened of the policemen.'

Mandy's mother knew he was right. 'But you're only eight.'

'He can come with me,' said the officer in charge, 'and help us look.'

At that moment there was a clanking as the street cleaner's barrow appeared, propelled along by two officers, one of whom held onto Lonnie's arm in a grip like steel. Dina felt blackness swirling around the edge of her vision. The PO grabbed her and lowered her onto a chair.

'Tea?' She took in the smudged mascara and lines of strain around Dina's eyes. 'You're not OK, are you?'

Dina shook her head. 'I lost my temper. I

shouted. Mandy ran off. She's so.... She's got poor comprehension.'

'Lonnie says that a girl in a balaclava pushed Mandy through a doorway round the back. Then the door slammed behind them!' said an officer.

'Kidnapped!' said Sidney with excitement. This was better than searching for any old wizards on The Edge. Better even than Dr Who.

A mug of hot sweet tea was pressed into Dina's hand. Even as she sipped and fumbled for a paracetamol, she wished it was a large glass of white wine. What had begun as a fun treat for both the children out in the city had turned into a nightmare that appeared to be growing out of control. She was trapped, unable to do anything.

Backstage Mandy swung her legs and the chair swivelled round and round. After a few minutes this palled and she realised she was bored. Then the door pushed open and Jazz flew in. In one hand she carried a can of coke and in the other a chocolate bar.

'This is all I can find, Mandy, for a snack.'

'Oh, thank you.' Mandy's lips parted and her extra-wide smile revealed uneven teeth. Behind Jazz stumped in a lady with grey permed hair and an apron tied around her ample middle.

'I'll sit with her, Jazz. You phone the manager. Her mother'll be doing her nut.'

Mandy put the can and the chocolate onto the counter amongst the hair-styling brushes, nail varnish, powder, lipstick and eye shadows. She pouted into the mirror, swivelled this way and that, and giggled. She caught Jazz's eye in the mirror as she wriggled up and down in the chair.

'You look like a Glitzy Girl.'

'Well that's because she...' began the old lady but Jazz held up her hand.

'I'm going to be busy in a minute, Mandy,' she said, 'but would you like to stand in the wings and watch The Girls?'

'The Glitzy Girls?'

'Mmm.'

'Oh yes,' she breathed, her eyes wide with excitement.

'OK then. Mrs. Parks'll get you seated. I'll just let the manager know you're here and he'll tell your Mum. We don't want her to worry, do we?'

'No,' said Mandy, her mind far away from any thoughts of how her mother might be feeling. All of a sudden though, she remembered her red-haired mother with her harassed expression and roughened hands. Her Mum was always there for her, sometimes cross, usually kind, always helping her: her mobile, her Facebook page and her car ever at hand.

'I've upset Mummy. Mummy'll be crying,' she called, her face flushed and her enormous blue eyes full of unshed tears. 'She'll think I'm dead! Gone for ever!' And she flung herself onto the floor of the dressing-room, beat the floor with her fists and howled.

Jazz crouched down beside her. 'Come on, Mandy. Let's go find Mummy for you. OK?'

Mandy scrambled up. She put her head in her hands and wailed loudly while real tears wetted her cheeks. The two women glanced at each other. Jazz noticed that Mandy was peeping between her fingers to see how they were reacting.

'She reminds me of my cousin,' she said. 'Both lovely girls. Beautiful faces. But not quite... "with it" like other ten-year olds.'

'Mmm.' Mrs. Parks tapped Mandy on the shoulder. 'Come on ducks. Drink up your coke.' She turned to Jazz. 'You go on. I can manage.'

Obediently Mandy drank, the storm of anxiety over almost as soon as it had begun. She shoved down the can which spilled a few drops amongst the diamante collars and several strands of black-coloured pearls.

'Does Jazz work here every night?'

'Yes, but...'

'Why does she wear a knitted hat?'

'Her head feels cold sometimes.'

'Does she always walk to work? Does she live with her Mum?'

'Yes. And her daughter.'

'Has Jazz got a baby?'

'Yes. But her 'baby's' five.'

'Does she go to school?'

'Yes. It's Special School.'

'Has her daughter got a disability?'

'Yes.' Mrs. Parks pulled herself together. 'Mandy, please hurry up or you'll miss seeing their act.'

Mandy immediately jumped up and pushed past Mrs Parks into the corridor. 'Which way is it?'

Eventually Mrs Parks got Mandy settled in the wings just as the band began to play. Suddenly the music was screaming loud and the stage full of long-legged girls in tiny sequinned skirts, microphones clutched to their mouths, long golden hair flying. A husky voice crooned and the beat thumped through the floor. Mandy lurched up and clutched her ears. Tears streamed down her face. She rocked her head from side to side, her mouth wide open in an unheard scream. Mrs. Parks didn't know what to do. Her mobile reverberated but she was too taken up with the child to answer it. Yelling and roaring pulsated from the audience.

At that moment a figure darted from the shadows. It was a boy with toffee-coloured eyes and slender jeans. He grabbed Mandy's arm and shook it hard. She stopped crying and clung onto him. He put her head against his chest and at the same time pulled her away from the edge of the stage.

'Come on, Mandy,' Mrs. Parks heard him say. 'Mum'll find us and she won't shout at you though she says her head hurts again.'

Mandy was a head taller than he was but she followed him, half falling over his legs, into the corridor behind. Round the corner emerged Dina, followed by the PC and the manager. By now Mrs. Parks was short of breath. Mandy flung herself at her mother.

'Mummy. Mummy I lost you!'

Dina hugged her daughter and stroked her hair. 'It's OK,' she kept saying. 'You're safe. Sidney's safe. And a lot of very kind people have helped us.' It would be useless she knew, to tell Mandy off. If she did there'd be a total meltdown. A huge amount of emotional energy would be expended without much to show for it. What she called 'the ice-pick' pain hammered dully behind her eyes. It was touch and go whether she'd pay for it later on in the evening. Everyone else safe in bed whilst she endured a migraine. Eventually they all ended up eating sandwiches and drinking tea in the manager's office.

'I'm sorry,' Dina kept saying. 'Mandy's got William's Syndrome. She can get very emotional and full of anxiety. And also she's hyper-sensitive to loud sounds.'

Everyone listened but no one answered. No one knew what to say, until the PC said, 'As long as she's been found, that's all that matters. That's what we're here for.'

By the time Jazz came across them during the interval, Mandy was yawning. She stared up at Jazz with little understanding in her blue eyes of who Jazz was.

'You that girl in the woolly hat on the steps?'

'Yes.'

'I saw someone who looked a bit like you on stage. Do you work here?'

It was Sidney who laughed. 'Mandy, Jazz IS a Glitzy Girl. She's got you a calendar and a DVD.'

But Mandy had lost interest. 'Mum, can I have another piece of cake?' she asked even as her thumb brushed the chocolate butter cream.

It was Jazz's turn to laugh. 'Dear Mandy! I wish all my fans were as nice as you!'

Dina sat back in her chair with another cup of tea and realised that her headache had begun to recede. Mrs. Parks shook her head over modern pre-teen girls. Sidney saw himself as the centre of attention in his Year Three class the next morning. The PC remembered that she was already halfway through her shift. Lonnie, free to go home now, left his barrow at the depot, straightened his back and took out a cigarette.

Meanwhile Mandy, oblivious to them all, glanced up at the perfect complexion of Jazz. 'Do you really know The Glitzy Girls? Have you got a baby? I mean a daughter? At a Special School? Has she got a disability? What's her name?'

Jazz laughed again. 'Just one question at a time, Mandy!'

'We need to get back home,' said Dina.

'Yes, it's time to go home now,' said Jazz. 'All good things come to an end. Goodbye dear Mandy. Ask your Mum, and you can email me.'

'Bye,' said Mandy and her blue eyes shone.

Beyond them the enormous blow-up figure of Santa Claus was suspended on the roof of the Town Hall, one boot forever locked into a replica chimney. The dreams and longings of thousands of city children fastened onto his sack of toys, while his plastic smile remained forever cheerful. All around him chimed the church bells of Christmas, calling with their wiser voices.

WIZARD IN WINTER

If he was ever going to meet a wizard, it would have to be today. Sidney snuggled down for several moments under the duvet and then stuck out his foot. It was chilly so he pulled it back and waited a few more seconds. Then he threw back the covering, leapt out of bed and put his nose between the curtains. The moon was still up, a silver thumbnail. But over in the east the sky flushed rose-pink. Soon The Edge would be out of its midnight-blue shadows and into the light. It was time to get up.

After breakfast his father said, 'Got your backpack? And make sure you put your wellies on.' So they set off.

In the carpark they met up with some other caving families coming on a ramble round The Edge. It was the winter solstice, or as it was more commonly known, the shortest day. Sidney saw Mark before Mark spotted him. He hoped that Mark wasn't in one of his, 'I'm older than you' moods, so when Mark scowled in his direction Sidney sighed. It wasn't a good start. Mark's grandma, known as Aunty Dora, had brought him along and she was wearing a thick woolly bobble hat pulled down over her ears. The bobble was pink and managed to look jaunty in the crisp morning air. Mark refused to wear the hat she'd brought for him and stumped along behind her with his head thrust down into his upturned coat collar. He wore no scarf and his hands were pushed deep in his pockets.

'Cocoa Stop!' shouted their leader, Don, a small man whose breath made a dragon-mist in front of his face and steamed up his glasses.

Aunty Dora pulled out a thermos and two plastic mugs, whilst Sidney's Dad searched in his backpack.

'Share ours?' she said. 'We've got plenty,' and she pulled out two more mugs, slim sachets of sugar, a plastic spoon and some ginger biscuits.

Sidney swirled the sweet drink around his teeth. Mark gave him half a grin and suddenly the day began to glow as the sun rose and made their eyes water. Sidney ran his finger over a rough sandstone outcrop and stared across the expanse of the Cheshire Plain towards Rainow and Lyme Park. He could see a few sheep, tiny in the fields below, and somewhere a dog barked.

'Once we get to Stormy Point,' said Don, 'we'll take a detour left to show the boys the wizard's well.'

Someone cheered.

Sidney kept his face quite still. 'Perhaps,' he thought, 'I'll meet a wizard today and have an adventure. I'll look into the spring waters and see a magic face.'

'It's a tall story,' muttered Mark at his side, with his Year Four superiority. 'There's no such thing as wizards!'

'Yes there is!'

'No there isn't!'

'Is!'

'It's a fairy tale. For babies.'

Sidney felt the dangerous tears well up. He blinked and clenched his fists, stepped away and hunched into his father's shadow. 'There's got to be wizards,' he thought, 'who know magical things and fight mythical beasts.' But perhaps Mark's right, replied a tiny voice in his head. Sidney dashed his hand across his eyes.

They rounded a corner and there was the wizard's well with the strange weathered stone face and rough-hewn lopsided writing.

Drink of this and take thy fill.
For the water falls by the wizhard's will.

Sidney crept forward and cupped his hand to drink from the murky water.

'Oh no you don't,' said his Dad. 'It's probably full of microbes.'

Sidney hung back after the others had continued their hike, to see if the stone face moved, or the letters changed to a new message without the spelling mistake. Nothing happened, though a blackbird sang.

'Come on, love,' said Aunty Dora, making Sidney jump. 'There's other mysteries to see today.'

'But Mark said wizards don't exist.'

Aunty Dora was silent. 'Maybe not,' she said at last, 'but there again it's easier not to believe.'

Sidney stared up at her. The pink pom-pom nodded like a crest on a strange garden bird.

Of all the grown-ups he knew, she certainly was the most surprising.

Their group gathered round Don, who said, 'We're on the way now to Engine Vein Mine.' He waved in the direction of a scar in the outcropping sandstone. 'It was first dug as surface pits in the Bronze Age, about 4000 years ago. They used stone hammers.'

The group fell silent as they contemplated the difficulty of doing this.

'Later on the Romans mined here and once we're underground you'll see where they dug. The passage is larger and squarer.' He turned, pressed open a small metal door half-hidden under the stones and disappeared. His muffled voiced floated back to them, 'It's quite safe if we all stick together. There are some lights as well.'

Sidney clung to his father's hand but they were quickly into the main walking passage with a short drop into the chamber below, which was covered from the open air by a concrete slab.

His eyes soon adjusted to the weak light and he looked around. It was hushed with gaping black holes that led away into nothingness, although Don said that they were entrances to other shafts and passages.

'Men from Neolithic times used stone tools to find the copper,' came Don's voice, echoing into the silence.

Sidney's eyes darted here and there. Somehow, he knew, just round the next corner, the wizard would be waiting in a dark woollen robe with silver moons embossed on it. His piercing eyes would bore into Sidney's soul and his hand would be ice-cold like steel. He would put Sidney into a boat and together they'd skim across a lake of darkness, deep under the Edge, to a cavern where King Arthur's knights lay sleeping until roused to help Britain in her hour of greatest need...

Mark pinched his arm and trod on his foot. 'Keep up, you naff-head or I'll get you,' and he screeched into Sidney's ear.

Sidney screamed. His father gave his arm good shake and Aunty Dora cannoned into him.

'Quiet!' called Don. 'There's a marvel here to see.'

Everyone stopped and gazed up at what looked like a sea-green waterfall frozen in time and motionless on the stone. Mark put out his hand to touch it and felt the rough surface and smoother malachite.

'Perhaps it's the wizhard's will,' he said and sniggered.

'You keep quiet, Mark,' said Aunty Dora in a sharp tone which Sidney hadn't heard her use before. 'You're being a pest.'

Sidney said nothing. The day was spoiled anyway. Perhaps Mark was right and it was nothing but sandstone weathered by rainwater seeping in, and the toil of ancient men to make a living.

'We'll soon be outside again,' said Don, 'and we can have our picnic.'

At that moment the lights went out. For a few moments there was total silence, broken by a little cry.

'Everyone, hold hands,' cried Don. Sidney felt his hand found by his father's and held in its warm grasp. On his other side a small cold hand fumbled for his and he took it and gave it a squeeze. Mark, he guessed.

'Stand quite still.'

The darkness pressed in on them. Sidney felt he could almost smell it, it was so thick. It was a world of anoraks, hand-clasps and a sudden acrid smell of sweat. Even if he turned his head he could see nothing. There was quite literally nothing. All the light was swallowed up.

'Our exit time is known. If we don't appear they'll send out a search party.'

Someone coughed and the air was fusty. A drop of water plopped nearby. Sidney jumped. All at once he sneezed and wiped his nose on his coat. His hand was free now and a lump trembled up in his throat making it tight. He felt in front of him with his hand but there was nothing. He turned round. Suddenly he didn't know which way to face, what path to take or how to get out. Darkness, like a thick black cloth, hung in front of him.

'Dad...'

Mark squeezed his other hand. 'I'm here,' he said in a tiny voice.

'We're lost...'

'No we aren't,' came Aunty Dora's voice.

Sidney could smell the damp earth and shivered. The ground remained hard beneath his feet. He moved his head and grazed his cheek on some rough rock.

'OK, son?' said his Dad and felt for Sidney's palm with his big firm hand clasp.

Then just as suddenly the lights came on again. A hubbub of conversation broke out.

'Must have been a power cut.'

'Follow me please. We'll go the shortcut back across the metal bridge.'

They stumbled down a steep descent of steps, crawled under a low boulder suspended above them and at last arrived at the entrance. Their leader took the key from a chain around his waist and each one stooped to leave. Just before they scrambled out Sidney turned round and caught sight of a man who seemed to be staring straight at him. The man's eyes reflected no light and peered through long, greasy black hair. Round his neck hung what looked like a fur collar. 'Strange,' thought Sidney, turning back towards the exit. 'Who on earth is he? I didn't spot him before.'

Outside Sidney and Mark gulped in great lungfuls of air. The light almost burnt their eyes. Never had a cold frosty morning been so inviting. They chased after each other, laughed and threw up piles of dead leaves.

'If being on your own in that darkness is where a wizard has to live,' thought Sidney, 'I'd think twice about it.'

It was after he'd dislodged a big pile of leaves that he caught the glimpse of something silver in the muddy ground near the exit from the mine shaft. He bent down, scrabbled in the soil and pulled out a ten pence coin. Without thinking he pushed it into his pocket. And there it remained for the rest of the day.

After the darkness underground most people wanted to go home and headed back to the car park. Sidney hung back but Mark was waiting for him. He stuck out his foot and Sidney crashed down onto the limestone-chatter pathway.

Mark ran on ahead shouting, 'Beat you to the car!'

Sidney hauled himself up and rubbed his knee. It hurt. His shoelace had come undone so he bent to tie it. But the more he tried, his cold, stiff fingers refused to get it into a bow. At last he'd done it and he looked around. Everyone had gone. He was quite alone. No one had waited for him. His so-called 'friend' Mark had turned out to be just the opposite.

Suddenly all the disappointments of the day crowded in onto him. He turned and rushed back in amongst the trees and headed back down the face of the escarpment, neither knowing nor caring where he went. The twigs of the trees whipped across his cheeks and his feet slithered under him on the scree-like surface.

'Don't care!' he thought. 'They can come and find me if they want me! I'll be better off on my own.'

A jet-black dog leaped out at him, snarling and barking, with flecks of spit shooting from its jaws. Sidney halted.

'Good dog,' he said and his voice wobbled.

The dog looked at him and ran behind his legs. Sidney tensed but the dog simply sniffed his boots, wagged its tail and whined. Sidney reached out and stroked its head. The hair was warm and silky. He tried to carry on but that made the dog bark in a frenzy. Sidney stopped and the dog stopped. Then it nudged him gently as if to say, that's the wrong way, turn back the way you came. So it was that, as Sidney climbed back towards the car park, the dog danced and wagged. But if he tried going downhill again it barked and snarled. Sidney gave in. He realised that the dog wasn't going to hurt him but had simply rounded him up and was treating him like a sheep being sent back to its pen, or in his case the car.

'Jasper! Come here boy!' A loud and friendly voice floated up the hill. Sidney turned round and saw a farmer with a red face standing at the bottom of the slope. 'You OK, young lad?' he called to Sidney.

'Yes, thanks to your dog!'

'Oh he loves rounding everybody up! But,' said the farmer, who'd climbed up the hill towards Sidney with massive strides, 'he doesn't take to everyone. He likes you.'

Sidney felt a glow somewhere deep in his chest. 'He was sending me back to the car,' he tried to explain, when round the corner of the track came the puffing figure of his father.

'Where've you been? I've been waiting and waiting!'

'Oh he's been helping with our Jasper,' said the farmer. Sidney's Dad adjusted his expression. 'We've had quite a day of it,' he began, 'what with being stranded down the mine with no light.'

'Well,' said the famer, 'come back to us for a cuppa tea and the missus'll show you Jasper's puppies. How would you like that!' He indicated Sidney who was out of his line of vision. 'Your young lad'll need something to take his mind off it. Not nice down there in the dark.' He cleared his throat. 'I went down there once with some big lads when I was about five. They ran off and left me. I were terrified. It was Jasper's 'Dad', Spot, what found me. Sniffed me out.' Farmer Colin shuddered. 'No wonder Jasper headed your boy back towards the car park!'

So it was that Sidney, his Dad, the farmer and Jasper all had a ride on a tractor. They ended up round a farm kitchen table with big mugs of tea and slices of cake. And in the corner in a cardboard box squirmed several squealing bundles of puppyhood. Sidney couldn't take his eyes off them. Farmer Colin took one and handed it to him. Sidney could hardly breathe for excitement, but quickly realised the puppy was strong and bold and needed a firm grasp. She was black all over with a few tiny white hairs on her forehead.

'Star, I'd call her,' said Farmer Colin. 'She's got that marking like a star on a dark night.'

'Yes,' whispered Sidney. 'Oh, yes.'

It wasn't until bedtime that Sidney put his hand into his pocket and found the silver coin again. He took it out and placed it on his bedside table. He'd put it towards an ice-cream sometime. He gave a great big yawn. His father looked in to say goodnight and picked it up.

'Now that's very old,' he said. 'Where did you find this?'

Sidney explained and his father listened.

'I reckon it's older than all the wizard stories,' his father said at last. 'You've found something really magical there, Sidney. You've found a real coin from a lost age. I wouldn't be surprised if it was Roman.'

'Roman?'

'Yes. That caver, Don, did say the Romans had worked that mine shaft we saw today.'

Sidney stared at the coin. 'Roman,' he kept saying. He grinned up at his Dad who ruffled his hair. Quite suddenly the day was right again. The wizard seemed to have shrivelled up to nothing much at all, while in his hand, catching the light, was a real piece of history.

'What a day,' said his Dad. 'You've seen a frozen green waterfall of malachite, found a Roman coin and met Star the puppy!'

'And seen a man with strange unlit eyes staring at me,' thought Sidney, but all he said was, 'It's been ace!'

His Dad examined the Roman coin in the palm of his hand.

'Quite a mystery to solve there, Sidney.'

Back down the mine, deep beneath The Edge crouched a Bronze Age miner. Lank, raven-coloured hair hung across his forehead and round his shoulders was slung a fur cloak. In one hand he held a flaming torch of oiled rags. He dug his other hand deep into a rounded pot full of coins and let them fall in a shining arc through his fingers. Their jangle was pleasing but his face was set in a frown.

The coin he'd hidden within the folds of his fur cloak was missing.

CHRISTINGLES

'Bet you'll never guess what I've got!'

Sidney glared. 'What?'

Mark sidled just beyond reach, half took something out of his pocket and then shoved it back again. He darted away amongst the gang of footballers in the playground and draped himself across the railings, trying and failing to whistle a tune. Sidney pretended not to notice. He gazed away in the opposite direction, heard the bell and sauntered up to his line. Mark's line was next to Sidney's and he dug his elbow into Sidney as his class filed past.

'Show you at playtime.'

Sidney put his nose in the air and stared straight ahead. At playtime it rained and so it wasn't until lunchtime that Mark was able to see Sidney again at the lunch queue.

'Hey Sid, look at this.' He thrust something small, hard and oblong into Sidney's hand. Sidney looked down at a mobile phone case with a picture of Spiderman on it. He could feel the mobile inside.

'Where d'you get that?'

'Wouldn't you like to know!'

'It's against the rules to have mobile phones in school.'

Mark stared at Sidney's freckled face. 'Rules! Is that all you're bothered about!' He stamped away from the younger boy and made for some older boys.

'What a baby,' he said loudly and clearly and

jerked his head in Sidney's direction. They all turned and stared back at Sidney who flushed and hung his head. One of them made a grab at Mark's pocket, pulled it inside out and the phone clattered onto the floor. Another picked it up and fiddled with it. The screen lit up.

'Pay as you Go! Ancient!'

'I've got the iphone6 at home,' said another.

'Spiderman!' They all sniggered and pushed past Mark. One of them casually dropped the phone back onto the floor and kicked it under the radiator. They headed out to the Year Six playground. Mark knelt down and scrabbled about until his fingers felt the phone. Somehow he managed to lever it along and eventually it re-appeared along with some fluff. The slip-case was jammed behind too but Sidney wormed it out for him and brushed the dust off. By this time though Mark had gone into the dining-room so Sidney pushed it into his pocket.

After lunch Mark wandered along until all at once he spotted Sidney. Suddenly the sight of Sidney's sturdy legs and spiky red hair made Mark clench his fists. 'I'll get him,' he thought, 'and make him sorry he's always saying he can read harder books than me!' Without stopping to think he raced across the playground and shoved Sidney hard until he fell over onto the tarmac. He pummelled Sidney in the chest. Sidney dragged himself off the ground and grabbed Mark's hair. The more he pulled the more Mark beat him. And the more Mark's fists bashed his chest the more Sidney pulled at his hair. Children appeared from nowhere and formed a circle around them. Shouting and jeering filled the air.

'Sidney! Sidney!'

'Mark! Mark!'

It was over almost as soon as it had begun. Support staff and the Head Teacher hauled them apart. They were marched into school

and made to sit at opposite ends of the corridor outside the Head's office. Parents were
telephoned. Their mothers arrived at school.
Detentions were set. Extra Maths homework
was doled out. No one listened when Sidney
tried to explain who had started the fight.

Mark's mother said, 'Boys will be boys,' and
groaned.

Sidney's mother didn't answer apart from to
say to Sidney, 'Just wait till you get home. I'll
tell your father.'

There was a slight pause and Mark's mother
looked away.

Sidney fared the worst, even though he hadn't
started it. There was to be no TV and no iPad
for a week. He had to go to bed early.

'Mark showed me a phone. And it's against
the rules.'

Sidney wailed and rubbed his face. His
mother made no further comment but shut
his bedroom door quietly.

Next day the two boys avoided each other. At lunchtime Sidney patrolled the playground, on his own as usual. Mark watched him out of the corner of his eye. The phone was still in his pocket. A teacher strolled up to Sidney at that moment and Mark half-turned away. She was smiling and suddenly Sidney was smiling and followed her into school. Mark watched them go. The playground felt bigger and emptier now Sidney had gone and it struck Mark for the first time that there was no one around for him to play with either.

In school Miss Baker said, 'Would you like to help us make some Christingles, Sidney?' He followed her into a classroom. There was a golden glow from the lights and he sat at a table with several older children. There was a pile of oranges at one end, some cocktail sticks, a box of dolly mixtures, some fruit pastilles and a packet of raisins. On a roll was some red, sticky cellotape.

Miss Baker held up an orange. 'This represents the world.' She reached for the red cell-otape. 'And this shows the suffering of Christ. Over here are candles which show Jesus as the light of the world.' She reached across Sidney for two dishes. 'And these are dolly mixtures that represent the good gifts of the earth.' The other dish contained sultanas and cocktail sticks. 'These are the four seasons.' She held up a completed Christingle for Sidney to see. 'We're making 100 of these for the school carol service tomorrow.'

'Oh,' said Sidney, who wasn't even sure he remembered when the school carol service was, never mind a special orange.

'At the end of the service we turn out all the lights and hold up our candle flames. It's a magical sight.'

He concentrated and watched the others. Christmas music played softly in the background and the older children showed him what to do. Gradually he settled into the rhythm of it and his shoulders relaxed. After a while he realised that Mark had somehow got in the classroom and was sitting next to him.

'Sid,' he whispered.

Sidney inclined his ear in Mark's direction.

'The phone case's gone.'

Sidney carried on without looking up. 'I'll keep my eye out for it,' he muttered, without giving eye contact. The case pressed into his thigh through his pocket but he ignored it.

Eventually a pile of Christingles had grown at the end of the table. The smell of orange peel scented the air and it wasn't only Sidney's fingers that were sticky with a taste of dolly mixtures and raisins.

It happened so quickly that no one knew who started it or indeed if it was an accident. One moment Sidney was sitting at the table, the next Mark got up, tripped over a chair leg, and his candle broke even as he crashed down on top of Sidney. Worse, Sidney's final

Christingle flew off the table and squelched down onto the floor in a squash of broken candle and split cocktail sticks. Sidney grabbed one and thrust it hard into Mark's hand.

'You beast! You've spoilt my Christingle,' he yelled, his face bright red and his body shaking.

Mark dragged himself up and rubbed his hand. Into the silence he said without looking at Sidney, 'Sorry.' Then he sucked his hand hard, put his half-finished Christingle in front of Sidney and walked out of the room. Sidney put his head down on the table and tried not to cry. The punishment on Miss Baker's lips died away.

'Come along,' she said at last. 'I don't think you're very well.'

When Sidney got home it was beginning to get dark. He pushed open the back door and his mother looked up from the ironing.

'Hi. You OK? You look a bit funny. Have you been crying?'

Sidney shook his head, took a biscuit and wandered into the front-room. Everything around him seemed far away. All he could think of was the jab into pink flesh, his determination to shut Mark up once and for all, to hurt him, 'forget' to tell him he had the phone case in his pocket. In his mind's eye he saw the purplish hole on the back of Mark's hand where the cocktail stick had punctured the skin. Mark's startled face and twisted mouth seemed to lurk around the corners of his vision. After a few minutes of staring past the TV set he walked back into the kitchen.

'Mum?'

'Mmm?'

'I've … had a quarrel.'

'Who with? Ah, let me guess. Mark?'

Sidney nodded and stared hard at the table.

'Did he provoke you?'

Sidney didn't answer.

'Well, do you think you should do anything?'

Sidney said nothing, but he looked up at his mother. Her voice sounded sharp but she had that kind look in her eyes.

'Could I take him...a book?'

'Why not?' She looked at the clock. 'Why not do it after tea and I'll come too? You'll feel a lot better then.'

Sidney turned and walked out of the kitchen. He ran upstairs and yanked any book off the shelf in his bedroom and stuck it under his arm. He tip-toed downstairs, then as quietly as he could, opened the front door and slipped out. He'd be back before his mother even realised he'd gone. He shot down the drive in the twilight and ran the five minutes to Mark's terraced house a few streets away. Once there his heart began to thump but he rang the bell and then bent his head as he heard the noise of someone coming. The door opened. Mark stood there and simply stared at him.

Sidney said, 'I've brought you a book. And I found the phone case.'

Mark pulled open the door and stood back for Sidney to come in. Sidney entered the hall and Mark shut the door. There was a strange smell, like old coats and dogs all mixed up. It took Sidney a moment to realise what was different about Mark's hall: there was no carpet on the floor, only bare stained floorboards, but not like the nice golden ones his mother had in their front-room. He shivered. Mark noticed.

''Sorry,' he muttered. 'The electric's off.'

Sidney stared at him uncomprehendingly.

Mark touched the radiators. 'They might come on later and warm the place up.'

'Oh.' Sidney held out the phone case with its faded Spiderman cover. 'Is this it?'

'Yep.'

'Right.'

Mark reached out for the case and Sidney saw his hand again, now with the puncture surrounded by some bruising. Mark saw his glance and said, 'It's nothing.'

'Yes, but…sorry.'

'Mum's out,' said Mark. He shrugged. 'Want a coke?'

'Yes, please.'

He opened the fridge and Sidney noticed it was quite empty except for three apples, some margarine spread and two cans of coke.

'Did you make another Christingle?'

'No, Miss Baker said there were enough.'

They sat together on the settee and drank the coke. It was very quiet in front of the blank TV screen. Sidney wished he'd remembered to bring his coat.

'Mum's got a job. At the Care Home. She won't be back for ages. I'm having toast for tea.'

'Mark, did you … borrow the phone?'

Mark fiddled with the can. 'Peter said I could. I'll give it back tomorrow.'

Sidney thought, 'The teachers'll know by then. They'll realise. Mark'll be in trouble.' He took a deep breath. 'Shall I take it back for you? It's Peter Gibbs's phone, isn't it?'

Mark got up and wandered in the direction of the door. 'OK,' he muttered and pointed to a shelf behind the TV set. He flung something behind it as he passed. At that moment car headlights flashed into the front-room as Mark's Mum drove up and screeched the brakes. Mark ran to the door. Sidney scrabbled behind the TV and grabbed the phone and found the case again. He managed to get them into his trouser pocket just in time.

Mark's Mum was in the hall. 'I've borrowed some coins,' she cried, 'for the meter.' Her face looked old and pinched. She spotted Sidney and put a smile into her voice. 'Hi. Do you want a coke?' In her hand was a plastic carrier bag with a sliced white loaf, some crisps and a bottle of wine.

'No thanks. I've got to go home now.' He

glanced at Mark who gave him a half smirk from behind his hand.

'See you,' he said.

'See ya.'

Sidney pulled the door closed behind him. He knew exactly what he was going to do but he hadn't bargained for the darkness and the tree branches waving in the wind above his head, like big hands sweeping down to grab him and squeeze him up. He ran. At first it was alright because Mark's street was lit with street lamps. But Peter Gibbs lived in a posh road nearer the Edge. Sidney felt very small and the cold seeped under his collar and made him thrust his hands deep into his pockets. Suddenly, into his mind came the memory of the happy half-hour in the lunchtime classroom with the Christingles and the golden candle-light, the sweets and the Christmas music.

'I've got to do it,' he thought.

Yet in no time at all he was running down Peter Gibb's drive and all the house lights blazed. He thrust the phone and the phone case through the letterbox and heard the dull thud from inside. Then he set off home. This time all the street lights had come on and in what seemed like a few minutes he was back at home, puffed, frozen and with the feeling that a heavy weight had been lifted from his chest.

He stumbled into the kitchen and was met by a blast of warmth.

His mother looked up. 'Like a scone?'

Sidney sat down at the kitchen table, stuffed the scone into his mouth and within five minutes was fast asleep, his head cradled on his arms. She ruffled his hair.

'Something's been going on, no doubt about it,' she thought. But as for what it was she guessed she'd never know.

THE ICE-CREAM MACHINE

Mark's brows furrowed. He leaped up from the settee. 'Come to the Christmas party? At the Care Home?'

'Yes.' His mother leaned forward. She'd feared he'd take it like this.

He shook his head and raised a hand as if to push the whole idea into the waste paper basket. 'No way!'

'But why not? It's warm and dry there and it'd be a bit of Christmas fun for you.'

'Fun?'

'Yes. There's the Salvation Army brass band coming to play carols at 4:00 o'clock and a wonderful party tea. Crackers and paper hats. A six foot Christmas tree. It'll be very nice.' Her voice was rushed. 'All the old dears ... ladies and old gentleman have heard about you.'

It was getting worse by the minute. Mark's mouth was round with horror. 'They're all in bed. Wearing nappies,' he shouted. 'I'm not going there!' And he flung himself towards the doorway.

His mother stood up. 'That's enough. Don't be so rude about them. There are some lovely people who live there.'

Mark hung his head. He could imagine the scene on the playground if any of the Year Six boys found out where he'd been. 'I'll be OK here Mum. I'll wait till you get back.'

But his mother marched straight past him into the hall where her feet resounded on the bare boards.

'You'll do as you're told, young man. You're not staying here on your own.' She snatched his coat off the peg. 'Get upstairs. Now. Wash your face. Clean your teeth. We're going in half an hour.' She flung his coat across the room with some force and it landed right where he'd been sitting. As he dragged himself up the stairs her voice beat on his back. 'You'll be grateful you've been invited. You're a very fortunate boy. At least I've got a job there even if it is only part-time. And if that means you've to show your face this afternoon, tough!'

'Yes, Mum.'

'And, although you don't deserve it, one or two of them said they might wrap up a present for you. So make sure you've got a smile on your face.' She slammed the lounge door. 'Right?'

'Right.'

At that moment the front door bell rang. She yanked it open to see a delivery van outside and a young man on the step who asked her to sign his delivery note. Jenna took the parcel. It was big and the weight made her stagger slightly. She dragged it across the floor and into the lounge. Then she looked closely at the postmark. From South Wales and addressed to Mark. That was unusual, but all her antennae were out. She scented trouble. If it was from whom she thought it might be from, then Mark could be even more upset than ever. He had already bounced downstairs again.

'Who was that at the front door? Anything for me?'

She knew it was too late to hide it from him as she would have done if he'd been younger.

'Let me see if you've done your teeth properly first.'

He bared his teeth at her and grinned.

'It's for you.'

'Me! Who from?'

She sighed. 'It's from an address near Cardiff.' Suddenly she had a brainwave. 'It must be a Christmas present, so let's put it under the tree. You can't open it yet.'

They pushed the box across the carpet until it came to rest next to what they called the 'tree'. This was more of a fir tree branch which Mark had found on the pavement near the greengrocer's on the High Street. He'd dragged it home and together they'd filled an old plastic bucket with soil and pressed the end of the branch in there. His mother wrapped some Christmas paper round the bucket and decorated it with some old-fashioned fairy lights and a few baubles left over from previous years. It stood, lopsidedly, near the TV and when Mark pressed his nose into the pine needles there was a scent of fresh pine woods and damp earth.

Now there was the big box next to it, plus a calendar he'd made her at school with a glittery star on it. The Christingle Miss Baker found for him sat on the middle of the table waiting to be lit on Christmas Day. So the lounge did look a bit Christmassy.

His mother said, 'I did wonder if it's from your father. He lives in South Wales.'

Mark stared at her uncomprehendingly. He was scarcely aware that he had ever had a father, although he did have a vague memory of rowing on a lake and eating a strawberry ice-cream with a man who had a big smile and a lot of black hair.

'My father?'

'It's a long time ago.'

'Do I have to go and live with him?'

Jenna's heart lurched. After all this time she still feared her son might be claimed back from her.

'No, I'm sure he won't expect that,' she said and forced herself to decipher the child's expression.

Mark said, 'Well I'm not going, I don't know anybody down there, I don't want to go to a different school and Mr Green says I can help with refreshments at the Charity Football match next term.'

Jenna's breath expelled in a gasp. So he didn't want to go and live with his father, or not at the moment anyway.

Mark was watching her. 'I'd rather come to the Care Home party with you, Mum, than go down to a strange place on a train by myself.' He actually shuddered.

She ruffled his hair and found she couldn't speak. He put on his coat and together they set off for the 20 minute walk to the Care Home. All the residents cheered when they saw Jenna arrive with Mark in tow. He hung back at first but she bustled about saying, 'Hello' to them all, put on her overall, got the after-lunch trolley organised and persuaded Mark to help with handing out the cups of tea.

A minibus rolled up outside in a splatter of gravel and the Salvation Army band climbed out with the curiously-shaped cases that contained their instruments. Mark suddenly wished he could play a drum or a trumpet and take centre-stage. He could hear Mr Godolphin, the manager, saying, 'Welcome' to them all, see them as they filled up the entrance hall, group themselves under the Christmas tree and start to tune up. The residents made a rough semi-circle. At last the band began with a medley of carols and Christmas songs. Mark glanced down the passageway towards the kitchen and caught a glimpse of Mr Godolphin holding up a bunch of mistletoe and attempting to persuade his mother to let him kiss her cheek.

'Weird,' thought Mark. 'Boys' mothers didn't usually giggle like that. They told you off about muddy shoes and watching too much TV.'

Everyone sang Good King Wenceslas at the tops of their quavering voices and one or two beat time. It was tea-time soon and Mr. Godolphin and his mother served plates of sandwiches, crisps, sausages on sticks, celery and cubes of cheese. The noise of laughter grew louder and louder. Mark grinned, talked, read out jokes, sang and ate until he felt stuffed to the eyeballs, which had been rare in his life.

One of the bandsmen said, 'Have a go with the trombone?'

Mark tried and couldn't coax a sound out of it.

'Not to worry. It's a special technique. But you've got a good sense of rhythm. You might be a natural at playing.'

When the residents had settled down to watch a Christmas film, Mr. Godolphin called Mark to his office.

'Well, young man, you've made their day.'

Mark didn't know what to say.

'You're a credit to your mother.'

Mark squirmed and blushed. 'Not always I'm not,' he muttered.

Mr Godolphin laughed. 'It's obvious to me that you're a really thoughtful boy.' He reached under his desk. 'That's why I brought you a special Christmas present.' He passed a large plastic bag over the desk to Mark. 'It's a "thank you" from me and from some of the other residents.' Mark took it and found it was heavy. 'There's something in it for your mother as well. She knows about it.'

Mark looked at the gangling figure of Mr. Godolphin in his old-fashioned suit, striped tie and smell of after-shave, his glasses and bald head, and realised for the first time that kindness wasn't necessarily the preserve of the young and beautiful celebrities who peopled the TV screen.

'It's our only presents,' he blurted out.

'I did wonder.'

'I made Mum a calendar at school as well.'

At that moment his mother put her head round the door, 'Mark, everyone wants to say 'Good-bye'. Oh, and Mr. Humble has got something for you.'

Mr. Godolphin interrupted by saying, 'Do you mean our latest resident?'

'Yes. I thought I hadn't seen him before.'

Mark looked over at a thin and wasted man sitting on his own in a corner who looked so wizened that Mark wondered if he was 100 years old.

'I'd like to give you this,' he said to Mark and delved deep into his pocket. Out he brought a fob watch without a chain. It rested solid and gold in his palm. 'It belonged to my grandfather and his before him.' He twiddled the winding mechanism at the top but the hands didn't move. He rubbed the watch face and looked across at Jenna. 'It needs some attention, but I'd like him to have it. He's been so friendly this afternoon it's quite cheered me up.' Jenna thanked him over and over again. 'It's gold,' she kept saying.

Mr. Humble slid his fingernail into a tiny groove and the back of the watch swung open like a door. Inside was a hallmark. 'Swiss made' it said, 'fifteen jewels'. He pressed another groove and an inner gold circular door opened, this time revealing cog after cog, and half-hidden cogs below, which moved the hands and indicated the hours, minutes, seconds. All around them the party noise whooped and shrieked but on their corner was silence.

'Wow!' breathed Mark at last. 'It's amazing!'

'Of course you can't see 'Time'.'

Mark stared, his face a blank.

Mr. Humble seemed to have drifted into his own dream world and spoke in a whisper. 'Perhaps Time exists in an eternal present before the Big Bang.'

Jenna shifted from one foot to another. She glanced at her watch. Mark frowned in concentration.

'Was that when the dinosaurs died out?'

'I had a dream once,' said Mr. Humble as if he hadn't heard Mark. 'I was in an old-fashioned dining-room and there was a big clock over the fireplace. Suddenly an owl flew in and settled behind the clock on the mantelpiece, almost hidden. Just one or two feathers poking out.'

'Like Harry Potter,' cried Mark, his eyes shining.

'Owl of Wisdom,' said Jenna brightly, before turning to Mark. 'Come on now. It's school in the morning.'

Mr. Humble sat bolt upright in the chair, his tweed jacket now several sizes too large for him, flopped open. 'Yes!' he said. 'Yes, Mrs. - er - . Wisdom sitting behind the face of Time'. He settled back, his teal eyes full of light. Then they closed and he began to snore.

Mark didn't know what to say but Mr. Godolphin took his elbow and said, 'Help me with all these bags will you, Mark.'

Then they were in Mr. Godolphin's car and soon back at their terraced house. His mother clutched a bag of goodies and a freezer bag with what she called a turkey crown.

'I over-ordered,' said Mr. Godolphin to the steering wheel.

Mark looked at the frozen lump of turkey and wondered why it would wear a crown like one of the Three Kings.

'Like to come in?' asked Jenna.

'No, thanks very much. Another time perhaps. I must get back to the Home. And don't worry about the watch. If Mr. Humble forgets and asks where it is I'll let you know!'

'Bye. Thanks.'

'Bye.'

The car chugged away and the two of them stood in the hall.

'It's warm,' cried Mark as he leaned against the radiator.

'Brilliant!'

'But...'

'I've managed to pay the heating bill. Mr. Godolphin gave me a loan against my paycheque.'

Mark stared at her blankly and shrugged. He yawned. They put the bag of food and left-overs in the kitchen and set the turkey to defrost. Mark took the bag of gifts into the living-room, took each one out and placed it with great care under the 'tree'. He caught sight of the big cardboard box again.

'Shall we ...'

'...open it?' She finished the sentence for him. 'Why not.'

They ripped off layers of paper, forced their way into the box.

'G.E.L.A.T...' Mark tried to read.

'Gelateria.'

'What's that?'

'An ice-cream maker.'

Mark was baffled. Jenna noticed the word 'discontinued' on a yellow sticker underneath. There were packs of dried fruits and dried milk powders, all out of the date-stamp, and a recipe book. Alongside them was a fearsome stainless steel contraption with a mixing bowl.

'What do I do with it?'

She was silent.

'It needs a freezer to make the ice-cream.' She sighed. 'We haven't got one.'

'No.'

There were two envelopes. She gave Mark his and he opened it. A Christmas card fell out. Inside he read, 'Ciao! From your father in Italy!'

Hers contained a letter. 'Oh!' she said. 'He's getting married. Taking over the business back in Italy.'

Mother and son looked at each other.

'He says he found this at the back of a cupboard. It's a good make but might need an adaptor plug.'

'Married?'

'To a lady called Flavia. Good luck to them, I suppose.'

'He doesn't want me to go and live with them in Italy?'

She took his hand to stop the sudden twisting of his wrists. 'No, dear. He doesn't want either of us.' And cutting off the maintenance money, she read on, silently, all of £50 a month. Her face was set.

Mark crept up and snuggled up to her. 'Never mind, Mum. You've got me.'

She gave him a hug. 'I'd rather have you a thousand times!' There was a pause. 'Shall we put it away in the kitchen for now?'

He nodded. Then he saw Mr. Godolphin's gifts now arranged under the tree.

'Tell you what, Mum, I'd rather have Mr. Godolphin's presents. I'll bet they'll be good.'

'I bet they will.'

'And Mr. Humble's watch. It's amazing!' he said and yawned. 'I've had an ace day, best Christmas party ever.'

In his bed later he said, 'Mum, do you think Mr. Godolphin likes you? And do you suppose Mr. Humble's a wizard? He looks old enough.'

But before she could even begin to frame some answers he'd fallen fast asleep.

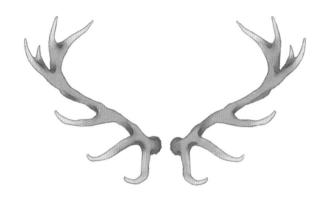

A REINDEER IN THE WINTER WOODS

Mandy listened. There it was again, a silvery, bell-like tinkle. She looked through the bare branches of the trees and down at the leaf mould under her feet. She stepped back onto the track and listened again. A delicate chime resounded, stopped, rang out, clear in the frosty air.

'Mum.'

There was no answer, only the crackle of her wellies on a frozen puddle. She peered back down the track behind her which led to the car park round the corner. Where was Mum? They'd been at the shops, met Dad, driven towards The Edge, called at the Garden Centre, then Mum said… what did she say?

'Don't forget The Challenge, Mandy. It's just after Christmas.'

Was that it? Mandy inspected her wellingtons, smoothed down the front of her pink furry coat. She shivered and pulled up her collar. So that was what she was doing, wasn't it? Practising her walking for The Challenge. She looked back in the direction of the car park. Perhaps she ought to…

'Whoa!'

She spun round and faced the woods. A sled jolted down the far track with a reindeer pulling it. What appeared to be an elf sat on the wooden seat and held the reins. Bells jingled on the harness.

'Whoa!'

Mandy stepped forward.

'Hi!' said the elf, who close up turned out to be a girl encased in an emerald green velvet costume which strained at the seams.

'Hello. What's your name? I've seen a picture like you at the Garden Centre.'

The elf-girl clambered off the sled and tethered the reindeer. 'I guess you were waiting for your ride?'

'Can I stroke him?'

'OK.'

Mandy raised her hand and brushed it down the reindeer's beige plump flanks. Brown eyes in a chocolate brown face regarded her and blew out a puff of breath that turned white in the chilly morning. He stamped a hoof and all the silver bells jumped and chimed on his red leather harness.

'Why are his antlers furry? He's not very tall is he? Are those silver studs on his nose-band?'

The elf-girl smiled. Her velvet suit was trimmed with white fur and she wore a Noddy-style pompom hat that encircled one shoulder. She offered her hand to Mandy who reached out to take it.

'Like your ride?'

'Yes, but…oh!…ouch!'

Something rested on her shoulder. A sand-papery tongue was licking the remains of breakfast cereal from round her cheek.

The elf-girl burst into a peal of laughter. 'Oh, Rudolf, you are naughty!'

'He's put his head on my shoulder.'

'Always on the look-out for a snack.'

Somehow, before she knew it, Mandy was hoisted up onto the sled and away they trotted down the track. The Cheshire Plain lay in a blue haze on their right and the dark wizard woods crowded to their left. They made a garish sight of pink fur, emerald green velvet and red leather on the home-made sled.

'Where are we going?' cried Mandy.

But the elf-girl didn't seem to hear her. They bumped on past grey trunks which soared to the sky in a canopy of bare branches which seemed like hands reaching down to grab at a young girl. A wind moaned and whistled occasionally in the tree-tops whilst Mandy clung on to a wooden bar that was rough with splinters.

At last the sled jolted to a stop. Mandy was half-flung off onto the dirt track. On their left were the crags and boulders of The Edge. A double metal track curved into the hillside. On it were two trucks and no engine. A metal door that led into the hill stood closed against the darkness. Mandy stared at it uncomprehendingly.

'That's a way into the old copper mines.'

She wrinkled her forehead and the reindeer shuffled in his harness.

'Men of long ago used to work with oak shovels far inside and sell the copper to the Romans.'

She yawned. 'Can I have an ice-cream?'

The elf-girl said, 'That bit comes later. At the Tea Rooms.' An edge crept into her voice. 'For now I'm showing you the sights.'

'Sights?' Mandy looked round but couldn't see anything.

'Sights…like the mine. And,' the elf-girl waved vaguely at the Cheshire Plain, 'the view.'

Mandy couldn't be bothered with the view. 'Where's Mum? Where are we going?'

The elf-girl took up the reins, Mandy stroked the rough beige fur and climbed back onto the sled.

'I'm cold.'

'You know where we're going next?'

'No?'

'Seeing where King Arthur's knights are asleep and then heading back to the Tea Rooms and some hot chocolate.'

Mandy's eyes gleamed. She yawned and sat obediently on the sled.

The elf-girl began to bite her lip. She took out a mobile phone. 'I'm on my way. But it's taking a long time. No. OK.' She looked over her shoulder at Mandy.

'You did win the prize, didn't you?'

'Prize?'

'Raffle prize. Trip round The Edge with an elf and a reindeer.'

Mandy's eyes remained blank and unfocused. 'I want Mum. I want hot chocolate. Where are we going?'

'Do you want to see the Wizard's well? And the site of the Armada beacon?' But even as she spoke the elf-girl knew that a trek up the Edge, onto the well and past the beacon, would be beyond Mandy's capabilities. The sun had disappeared behind steel-grey clouds and a spatter of freezing rain hit their cheeks. She took the bridle and led the reindeer on through the woods, without speaking; while Mandy bumped, swayed and rubbed the tears from her eyes.

'Stupid kids,' muttered the elf-girl to herself but Mandy didn't hear.

All at once as they rounded the track that led back to the car park Mandy noticed that now the metal door leading into the hill stood open. Beyond it was darkness.

'Look!' she cried and pointed.

But elf-girl was in a sulk and stomped along. Mandy lost her balance and half-fell sideways. The reindeer kicked his heels and began to trot. At the same moment a dog shot out from amongst the trees snarling with bared teeth. Mandy shrank into her coat, he leaped up at the sled, his coat as black as night. Somehow, between the dog and the reindeer, Mandy fell onto the gravelly ground, just missing the iron rails of the tram track. She screamed. Elf-girl yelled. The dog barked in a frenzy, then backed off with a growl.

Elf-girl shouted at Mandy, 'Get up! You'll have to walk.' She set off again, jerked Rudolf and dragged the sled forwards with her other hand. The dog panted and wagged his tail at Mandy. He nudged her shoulder, as much as if to say, 'Come with me. I'll look after you.'

'Come on!' yelled elf-girl. 'I've not got all day.' She marched on towards the bend in the track. Mandy scrambled up, looked down at her torn tights and bloodied knees and pouted.

'I'm not coming,' she muttered to herself. 'I don't care' and she flounced in the direction of the now-open metal doors. Meanwhile the jet-black sheepdog did a sort of dance around her legs.

Without quite knowing how or why, Mandy found herself inside the old copper mine with a dog trotting alongside her, fierce barks now forgotten. The memory of elf-girl, grazed knees and Rudolf faded whilst a wet nose touched her hand. Once she turned back and saw a mouth of light at the tunnel entrance. On the walls were torches that flamed and showed the path downwards deep into the hill. Ahead there was an eerie glow. Eventually they came to a chamber with several paths off, all pitch black.

Then the dog growled softly. They both stopped and pressed themselves into the shadows. Unseen but unmistakable was the sound of talking from far ahead, that echoed slightly in the chamber. The scrape of footsteps padding towards them and an occasional jangle made Mandy's breath come in a gasp. The dog pressed against her.

Several men crowded into the chamber. They squatted on their haunches and spoke in bursts of what sounded like Welsh. One man stood straight. He carried an empty sack. Over his shoulder hung a leather pouch and the jangle came from inside as his fingers played with the contents. His tunic was short, round his waist hung a scabbard with a sword and on his head was a helmet with a plume. When the others stood up Mandy saw they were dressed in furs. One had red hair tied back in a thong. The other two were raven-haired and expressionless, one very tall.

Eventually helmet-man gave the jangling pouch to red-hair who poured the shining coins into an earthenware pot. He passed it behind him to the others and its weight made them stagger. The tall miner tried to snatch it to himself and pull the pot into the folds of his cloak. The other gave a hoarse cry and grabbed at the tall miner's throat. Words split the air. Fists flew. Red-hair whipped round and shouted. Tall-man's face grew sullen in the shadows. Helmet-man's hand moved and rested lightly on his scabbard. Suddenly tall-man slumped down and the pot fell awkwardly.

It dropped onto the stone and broke the rim. Red-hair yelled. They righted it at once. In turn red-hair and the other miner emptied their stores of copper ore from their skin pouches into helmet-man's sack. At last tall-man pulled himself up and shoved his store of ore into the sack as well, where it settled with a dulled scrunch. There was silence. Then helmet-man shook his sack, hoisted it onto his back and all raised their hands in salute.

The miners melted away back down a path into the dark. Helmet-man strode towards the entrance, past Mandy and the dog so closely that her nose wrinkled in the pungent smell. As she watched his back, suddenly, he vanished. One moment he was there, the next he was gone. Then the horror of the darkness and flickering shadows hit her.

'Mum,' she cried and felt the dangerous noisy tears begin.

The dog leaped up beside her and tried to put his paws round her waist. 'You're hugging me,' she whispered and dashed the tears away. They set off almost at a run and before she knew it she was outside again, with elf-girl's emerald green costume ahead of them and about to disappear down the track. The dog gave a friendly, 'Woof!' and shot off amongst the birch trees. Mandy stumbled on while elf-girl waited for her.

'I've seen something strange,' she began. 'Maybe King Arthur and some…knights?' But what had she seen? Somehow none of it made sense. She noticed that in her hand she grasped a fragment of pottery. She stared at it, nonplussed.

At the car park Dina and Simon glared at each other.

'You said you'd look after her!'

'Yes. But she said she wanted to see the clothes. So I thought you'd got her.'

'But I never saw her!'

'I sent her across the floor towards you. She saw you!'

'That means nothing,' Dina shouted. 'She gets distracted and...'

'...wanders off,' said Simon.

'Well you never look after her properly. It's always me!'

'You never listen. She's given far too much freedom.'

Dina flung herself back into the front of the car. She pulled out her mobile.

'Look, who are you dialling now?' He wrested the car door open.

Dina put her head in her hands. After a moment he put his hand on her shoulder.

'Look, it's neither of our faults.'

'But where is she?'

'Perhaps she got a lift up here with The Browns. They were following me up here in their car.'

'You were too busy gazing at that special offer for Spring bulbs to take any notice of your daughter.' But the sting had gone out of her words.

They glanced round the car park. An empty stall had a banner which read, 'Have a ride with Rudolf and Esmeralda the Elf Princess.'

'I don't know. I expect they dropped her and said, "There's your father", and so she wandered off.'

The wind blew a flurry of hail and stung their cheeks.

'She could be anywhere,' said Dina staring across at the acres of woodland, tracks and trees. Simon got out his mobile.

'I'm dialling 999.'

'But that'll be the second time this week. Remember The Glitzy Girls concert.'

Dina shivered and Simon put his arm round her. They stood together for a few seconds.

'Come on,' he said at last. 'We've got to stay strong. For her.'

'And for Sidney.'

'Yes.'

He looked at his wife and saw the circles of exhaustion under her eyes, her unwashed hair, the frown marks between her eyebrows, the hastily applied foundation which left a tidemark of colour round her chin. 'We can't go on like this.' he thought.

Aloud he said, 'Come on. We'll spend half-an-hour looking for her and then call the Police.'

Back on the track the elf-girl spoke. 'I know, let's wait at the carpark.' She tugged at the bridle but Rudolf stopped. Mandy looked up. She managed to haul herself off the sled and rubbed her knees.

'I'll walk. I'm supposed to be doing The Challenge and practising my walking. That'll give Rudolf a rest from pulling me. Can I hold the bridle?'

The elf-girl was silenced by this abrupt change of emotion. They trudged back down the track. The first few snowflakes began to fall.

So it was that as Simon and Dina rounded the corner they saw Mandy immediately. Dina called and waved while Simon snapped them walking forwards on his mobile phone. Snow was falling on his daughter's dark curls, a reindeer trotted with muffled hooves and shook his red harness and all the bells. The elf-girl's pink cheeks glowed under her green velvet hood. However all Mandy did was to walk away from the elf-girl, forget to say good-bye, and leave the reins trailing on the ground. She flung her arms round Dina.

'I'm glad I found you, Mum. Can I have some hot chocolate? Mum, I've done lots of walking for The Challenge. And I might have seen King Arthur. And I found this.' She held out the broken pottery shard.

Simon took in the expression of the elf-girl's face and hastily paid her off. 'Sorry,' he mumbled. 'Crossed wires and all that.'

But what the reindeer thought, no one ever knew, although he could be seen pawing the ground, uncovering some grassy roots and bending his head to munch. In spite of the wildness and an open mine shaft door, Mandy was back safe again, with a piece of pottery to show for it. While all around them, unperceived and unrecognised, as silent as the gentle snow, fell a kindly and protecting grace.

A WICKER BASKET

Sidney woke up. The duvet felt heavy at the end of his bed, so he wriggled a toe and there was a rustle. After a second he leaped out of bed and raced for the light switch. Father Christmas had been! However hard he tried to keep awake, it was the same every year. He always missed the magic moment. There were the usual things in his stocking: chocolate coins, a satsuma, a few fun games. There were three further parcels, all wrapped in Christmas paper which he tore off. An Annual, a DVD and a new hoodie; he wanted them all...but it didn't seem...very much...He wrenched open his bedroom door.

'Mandy!' he yelled.

The light was on under her door, which he pushed open and half-fell into her room. The floor was covered in a sea of paper and there were even more Santa-presents on her bed. His eyes swept across them: a sequinned skirt, sets of books, a new phone, a phone case, DVDs, a shocking pink handbag, tights in lacy cream, a grey coat, chocolates, games, two jigsaws. Sidney became quite still. He brushed his hand across his face once. By the time Mandy looked up her brother had gone.

Sidney crept downstairs. There was a weight in his chest as if he were going to cry, or run away and hide. He heard a shout from his Dad but he carried on into the kitchen, not really sure what he was going to do in there. He sniffed. Already there was a smell of roasting turkey. He wandered into the middle of the room and stubbed his toe on something. He looked down. At his feet was a wicker basket he hadn't seen before. There was a glittery label on it which said, 'Sidney'. He reached to open the basket and noticed the side bulging. Then the whole thing rocked from side to side and he heard a squeak. He threw himself down onto the floor and undid the lid. Inside was some hay and a water bottle and .... a squirming, black-haired body, a thumping tail and a few white hairs on her forehead. The puppy yelped at him and launched herself upwards. Sidney picked her up and cradled her.

'Star!' he breathed.

'Amazing what Father Christmas can get down the chimney,' came his father's voice behind him.

Sidney couldn't reply but his shining eyes said it all.

'A friend for life.'

The puppy wriggled to be put down and began to sniff determinedly behind the table.

'Quick! Take her out.'

Sidney carried her outside and she wetted the grass. It was only once he was back inside the kitchen that he realised his feet were icy cold and he was shivering.

'Get your dressing-gown on.'

'A dog of my own, someone just for me,' thought Sidney.

'Farmer Colin says he'll help you train her.'

'Brilliant!'

All over Alderley children were opening their presents with excited cries. Mothers basted turkeys, fathers eyed the bottles of beer and wine. At church the nave was filled with straw and a lady, specially paid for the occasion, waited with a real live donkey to bring her in to the Christmas morning service. Carol singers tuned up, Mandy tried on her new outfit, old Mr. Humble dozed peacefully in the Care Home

and Mark sat back on his haunches, over-
whelmed by all his gifts of new jigsaws, books
and DVDs. The ice-cream-maker remained forgotten in the cupboard while Mark's mother,
Jenna, sat in silence. On her knee was a blue
velvet box with a gold necklace inside.

Next day, Boxing Day, Sidney crept downstairs again at first light. He muttered something at his parents' bedroom door and a
grunt could be heard in response. He stole
into the kitchen in his stocking-feet, grabbed
a backpack and stuffed some hay in the bottom. Next he found a muesli bar and some
dog biscuits plus a carton of orange and a
bottle of water and pushed them into the
side-pockets. Star squeaked. He opened her
cage, picked her up, carried her bodily to
the backpack and sat her inside its depths.
Her head poked out and he kissed her nose.
Then he let himself out into the back porch.
The cold air outside made him gasp so he

dragged on his coat and a woolly hat, and hoisted the backpack onto his shoulders. They were off.

He took the quarry path up to the Edge and skirted Farmer Colin's house. Red sandstone crags jutted out here and there. Sure footed, he clambered up the steep track towards the crest of the Edge, shivering in the deep shadows, dead holly twigs and shrivelled beech leaves crunching under his boots. If he could only get to the metal exit door of the Engine Vein where he'd found that silver coin the week before, he might find another one. Somehow he'd felt an urge to come this morning. The mile or so of climbing, followed by the walk along the flat path passed in a trice. The sun was higher now and warmer and he guessed it was about nine o'clock.

There was a smell in the air of woodsmoke and the odd shout. Star was wriggling to be let out so he bent down and set her free for a run, enticing her back with the dog biscuits and pouring some fresh water out for her into a rocky hollow in the track. His head was down and he searched with his eyes for silver coins. He kicked back the drifts of leaves and looked. But there was nothing. He rounded the corner of the track and saw the bare outlines of the stony Engine Vein fault, with the delves and scoops in the rocks. Some Scouts were sitting on their haunches round a campfire, almost blending with the rocks as if their legs were growing out of the boulders. Sidney shrugged. It must be a trick of the late dawn light, while his own spindly shadow curved lengthways across the sandstone. Star had run back to him and cowered near his legs. He bent to pat and reassure her and when he looked up again the scouts had melted away, leaving a scroll of smoke in the air. Sidney stared and frowned. He set Star down again and noticed an oddly smoothed stone on the ground with a 'waist' which fitted, rounded, into the palm of his hand. Star whined, snuffed and trotted forward. He followed.

A voice came, speaking something like Welsh. Over by the fire stood a couple of young men, one tall with raven-black greasy hair. There was also a lad standing apart from them who looked across and let his gaze fall on Sidney. Their eyes locked, brown to brown, and the lad's hair flamed red like Sidney's, only it was long and twisted back by a thong. He wore a tunic and animal skins for shoes. Sidney stopped, mesmerised. He could neither step forward nor run away. Star snuffled, jumped and half-fell out of his arms. She lolloped forwards, sniffed towards the lad's hand and barked, a tiny first bark. The lad laughed, a generous chuckle that filled the air and he held out his hand to her. He inched forward, knelt down and touched her starry forehead. He placed down a rounded, waisted-stone carefully as she touched him with her wet nose. He stroked her and then spoke to Sidney, who didn't understand at first. The lad pointed to Star, spoke again.

'It's Star,' Sidney said at last. 'She's called Star.'

'Star,' came the guttural reply.

Sidney smiled and the freckled, strong face smiled back. At that moment a plane roared overhead, Sidney looked upwards momentarily. By the time he looked back, perhaps in a couple of seconds, the lad had gone, as if he'd never been. Sidney stared out across the Engine Vein, pierced by sadness and longing, bereft of someone he'd known could be a friend.

Another voice came in his ear. 'Can you smell woodsmoke too?' It was Aunty Dora, complete with woolly hat and pink pom-pom.

Sidney nodded.

She said, 'I see them sometimes. Always working, toiling for the copper and lead.'

'I don't get it,' said Sidney. 'Who are they?'

She shrugged. 'Sometimes I wonder if Time doesn't go in a straight line,' she said at last. 'I wonder if it's curved. Or in a pleat. So if something or someone 'happened' long ago it might mean you were quite close to it or them and you could just reach out and touch...'

Sidney's head almost hurt with trying to work it all out. 'You mean they're Bronze Age men? But how come I saw them? I thought they were the Scouts.'

She shook her head. 'I simply don't know, dear,' she said. 'And I'm not sure what time of history they might be from. Perhaps Bronze Age if they were mining for copper? Late Roman period? But I'll tell you one thing. I never seek them out.'

'That red-haired one spoke to the puppy. He said "Star" to her.'

She smiled. 'Who knows? Perhaps one of the Romans they sold copper to, told them about a marvellous star in the heavens, which passed over even before they were born. Perhaps one of the legionaries talked to them about Christmas at a time when Christmas wasn't known or understood.'

'But they were like Bronze Age people.'

'But don't you think they were just like us too?'

Sidney's brow crinkled. 'He had red hair. Like me.'

'Well, who knows? Red hair can be passed down by genes. And your family has lived round here for years and years.'

They began to laugh, it all seemed so unlikely.

'And what's that in your hand?'

Sidney looked down at the strangely rounded stone which fitted into his hand like a glove. He ran his thumb across it.

'It looks very much like a Stone Age hammer. People do come across them sometimes.'

'One of the hammers from the Bronze Age mine workers?'

'Yes. Maybe it is.'

'Well the lad I saw with the fur shoes, he had a stone like this in his hand.'

Aunty Dora listened and thought. 'Do you think it's the same one?'

Sidney looked down at it. 'I don't know. But I found it nearby.' He pointed a few metres away to the pile of leaves at the edge of the track.

'It could well be, then. I guess we'll never know.'

They stood in silence for a few moments even as the smell of woodsmoke faded to nothing.

'I'd better get back,' said Sidney suddenly. Mum'll wonder where I am.'

Aunty Dora shivered suddenly and pulled down her woolly hat until the pom-pom was almost level with her eyebrows.'You've been granted a marvellous gift this morning, Sidney,' she said. 'Like a vision. Be careful who you talk to about it. And,' her grey eyes glinted behind her glasses, 'don't forget. The Giver is always more important than the gift. Always let the gift direct you to the Giver. You'll understand it all one day. I promise.'

'But who is the Giver?' he wondered, even as Aunty Dora prepared to carry on with her walk. She raised a hand in farewell. He watched as she strode off, her pom-pom dancing and her stick beating time on the path. Then he set his face for home. As he passed Mark's house he wondered about calling in and showing off Star. He hesitated. The memory of their fights and the jabbed cocktail stick burnt into his mind. But as he wondered what to do the front-door flew open and Mark himself shot out.

'Hi Sid!' he called. 'Want to see my jigsaws?'

'OK,' said Sidney, 'but I can't leave Star outside.'

Mark wasn't in the mood to take much notice of a sleeping puppy in a backpack. Sidney followed him in, and put the backpack down near the radiator. Inside the front-room were several jigsaws on the table and on the floor. There was a small pile of DVDs, a few books and The Star Wars annual, all with bright shiny covers. Sidney was startled.

'Wow!' he said, 'what fantastic presents, Mark.'

Mark couldn't wipe the grin off his face.

'Where d'you get them all?'

'Mum's friends at the Care Home. And,' he patted his pocket. 'Mr. Humble gave me a gold watch.'

The two boys examined the elderly and beautiful fob watch with its intricate face and hands which pointed to the seconds of time.

'Amazing,' breathed Sidney. 'Fantastic. I'll bet it's valuable.'

Mark's face was pink and his eyes shone. 'Want to come with us to the Recc after?' he asked. 'The others said you can come. I asked them.'

'Yeah,' said Sidney, as if it were the most normal thing in the world for a boy in Year Three to be invited to play with boys in Year Four. 'Sure do!'

Mark slung his arm briefly round Sidney's shoulder. 'Great! See you later. Oh,' he nodded towards Star. 'Ask your Mum if the puppy can come too.'